APR 1 7

☑ **W9-CQQ-444**

SPOOKY SLEUTHS

Read them all . . . if you dare.

The Ghost Tree
Beware the Moonlight!
Don't Go Near the Water!

SPOOKY SLEUTHS 3

Don't Go Near the Water!

Natasha Deen

illustrated by Lissy Marlin

A STEPPING STONE BOOK™
Random House 🏠 New York

Text copyright © 2023 by Natasha Deen
Cover art and interior illustrations copyright © 2023 by Lissy Marlin

All rights reserved. Published in the United States by Random House Children's Books, a division of Penguin Random House LLC, New York.

Random House and the colophon are registered trademarks and A Stepping Stone Book and the colophon are trademarks of Penguin Random House LLC.

Visit us on the Web!
rhcbooks.com

Educators and librarians, for a variety of teaching tools, visit us at
RHTeachersLibrarians.com

Library of Congress Cataloging-in-Publication Data is available upon request.
ISBN 978-0-593-48893-5 (trade) — ISBN 978-0-593-48894-2 (lib. bdg.) —
ISBN 978-0-593-48895-9 (ebook)

Printed in the United States of America
10 9 8 7 6 5 4 3 2 1

This book has been officially leveled by using
the F&P Text Level Gradient™ Leveling System.

For lovers of spooky stories —N.D.

To my family. Thank you for
your support. —L.M.

The bus stopped at the Lion's Gate Sea Research Center. My class was going to learn about the local ecosystem. Our task was to record the plants and animals we saw, then write a report about one of them.

I joined my friends Rokshar Kaya and Max Rogers near the water's edge. The building was behind us, but the mist hid it and made the morning damp and gray. Max shivered and pulled the collar of his coat close.

I shivered, too, but not because of the

cold. Lion's Gate, Washington, was the spookiest place I'd ever lived! Strange lights shone in the sky, people disappeared into the mist—even the water was creepy. It was endless, and the fog made it impossible to see below its surface. Every wave seemed to roll closer, as if trying to catch hold of our feet and drag us under.

Max and I were sure the town was home to supernatural creatures. Rokshar thought it was spooky because of secret projects at Eden Lab, the research facility where our parents worked. She figured the strange events were science experiments running wild. So far, we hadn't been able to prove either of our theories.

The bus driver honked his horn good-bye as my dad and Max's uncle Nelson exited. They were helping to chaperone our trip.

Dad came over and put his hand on my shoulder. "When I was a kid, I used to go sailing with my dad. I can't wait to be on the water again."

"I've been so busy working on the research center's renovations, I haven't done any of their boat tours," said Nelson. "I'm excited!"

I wasn't. Monsters like krakens lived in the water. On my left, the sea began to bubble. The tip of a fin appeared. I edged away.

Dad and Nelson, though, walked near the waves. "Cool things wash up onshore," Dad called to me. "Come look!"

"I'm okay!" I said, and hoped I didn't sound scared.

Nelson picked something up and showed Dad. They seemed excited, and I was curious. I started for them, then froze

as a growling roar echoed across the water. My ears tingled. So did my heart.

"Wild, hey?" said my teacher, Mx. Hudson, as they came up to me. "There must be a group of sea lions around the bend. They sure make a racket!" Mx. Hudson turned to the group. "Everyone, please gather in. This is Captain Hoxha." Mx. Hudson gestured to the tall, blond woman next to them.

She smiled and waved.

"Captain Hoxha is going to give us our

safety review. Then we'll head onto the boat for a tour around the island," said Mx. Hudson.

Unease trickled down my neck. Last week, my friends and I had seen a ghostly shape moving across the sand. When we investigated, there was no one around. There weren't even footprints. Just thinking about it made my skin crawl. What if that something was still out there?

After the safety review, Dad and I put on our life jackets.

I started to ask Dad what he and Nelson had found, but Dad nudged me and asked, "What did the sea say to the sailor?"

I shrugged.

"Nothing," said Dad as we boarded, "it just waved."

I groaned.

He laughed.

Max crossed his fingers. "I hope I see a killer whale."

"Me too," said Rokshar.

Captain Hoxha motored to a cove on the island.

"Record the plants and animals you see," said Mx. Hudson.

My friends and I saw a bald eagle and a warbler, but no whales.

Rokshar pointed to the cliffside. It stood to the right of the research center. In front of it, the water had turned orange-red. "Look, it's a harmful algal bloom. That's what happens when there's an overgrowth of phytoplankton." She looked over the railing. "There's some on the boat's hull."

"Is it dangerous?" I asked.

"Sometimes," she said, "but we're not touching it or anything."

"Wait a second," said Max, twisting around. "Where did my uncle and Asim's dad go?"

We found them at the rear of the boat, hunched over the railing.

Dad turned when I tapped him on the shoulder. His face was pasty, and his red hair stuck to his forehead. "I feel horrible," he said. "It's been so long since I've been sailing, I have seasickness."

"Me too," said Nelson.

"Sitting inside the wheelhouse might help," Max suggested.

They headed there.

Captain Hoxha started the engine and slowly set out for the next stop. I looked over the railing at the breaking waves. That's when I saw it: the pale face of a woman staring up at me. She was in the water and trying to climb onto the boat!

I grabbed Max. "There's someone under the water!"

He looked over the railing. The woman scowled at us. Max called Rokshar over.

"Oh my gosh!" she said. "We should get Mx. Hudson before the seal leaves. I bet it's curious about our boat!"

Seal? Max and I peered over the railing. A small seal stared back at us.

"No," I told Rokshar. "It was a woman!"

"She had long brown hair," Max added.

My stomach churned. "She might be

that ghostly figure we saw floating on the beach last week."

"That's definitely a seal," said Rokshar.

"I'm sure it was a person," I said.

Max nodded.

"When light hits water, it bends. Maybe the refraction made the seal look like a woman." Rokshar's hair whipped in the wind. "Anyone swimming underwater would need breathing equipment. It would cover their nose and mouth."

"Maybe," I said, but I knew what I'd seen.

Rokshar and Max walked to the wheel-house. I gave the seal one last look. Behind it, a gigantic, bright green fish tail rose from the sea, slapped the waves, then disappeared into the water. The seal barked and swam away.

What kinds of fish are bright green, big, and live in the Salish Sea? I couldn't think of any. Rokshar and I were keeping track of weird things that happened in Lion's Gate. We agreed to use the scientific method so our records were similar. A disappearing woman under the water and a mysterious fish needed recording!

Captain Hoxha slowed as we neared

our second stop. I wrote my observations in my journal.

* Last week, my friends and I saw a ghostly figure floating on the sand.
* Today, a woman was under the water and following our boat.

Step one of the scientific method was to ask a question.

* Why was she doing this? Is she connected to the ghostly figure?
* The only bright green fish I know live in tropical waters. Why is there a giant one in the Salish Sea?

I thought about what I'd seen and the stories Dad had told me about our Scottish heritage. I added my hypothesis, which was step two.

Selkies are sea people who can transform from seals into humans. My hypothesis is that the woman is a selkie.

As I was putting my journal back into my bag, there was a loud *bang* and the boat tilted to one side. Some of my classmates screamed. Others slipped and fell on the deck. I slid but stayed on my feet. Fear made my mouth dry.

"Stay calm!" Mx. Hudson yelled. They stood on the other side of the boat from me. "Hold on to the railing and make your way to the wheelhouse!"

Another metallic *bang* rang out. The boat lurched. I slipped. My knees cracked against the ground.

"What's happening?" cried Sydney.

"Just a strong wave," said Mx. Hudson. "Calmly come to me!"

I hurried toward my teacher.

"Don't run, Asim," said Mx. Hudson.

I slowed down. There was a final, terrible *crack* as something hit us again. The boat tipped to the water's edge!

Panic tightened my throat. Someone grabbed hold of my shoulder.

"You're safe," said Mx. Hudson.

My legs felt rubbery as I followed Mx. Hudson to the wheelhouse. I joined Max, Rokshar, my dad, and Nelson with the rest of my class.

"I'm sorry," Captain Hoxha said. "There's a storm approaching. It's causing higher-than-normal waves. We're heading back to shore early."

Dad placed his hand on his stomach. "I don't mind. I feel terrible."

Nelson started to say something. Then his face turned green. He pressed his palm to his mouth and looked away.

Captain Hoxha smiled at Dad, but her eyes narrowed as she looked at the water.

"I don't think it's a storm that's making us return to shore," I whispered to my friends.

Rokshar nodded. "Something

attacked the boat. When we get back, let's inspect the hull and see if we find any clues."

When we got to land, we looked hard. There were scratches from the boat scraping something, but no dents.

"Any real damage must be under the water," Rokshar said as we walked from the dock and

stood near the water's edge. "Too bad. I would've liked to know what came after us." She sighed, took out her journal, and started writing.

I thought about the lady and the giant fish. Neither of them seemed strong enough to toss the boat around, but my gut instinct was in overdrive. It said something dangerous was in the water.

Normally, I would have wanted to investigate. But the sea scared me. I was happy to leave this spooky thing alone.

The water a few feet in front of us began to churn. Bubbles rose to the surface. The waves foamed. I squinted. In the middle of the froth, a hand reached out to us.

3

I stumbled backward and fell. Max bent to help me. Rokshar moved toward the water.

"Be careful!" I yelled. "I saw a hand. It was reaching out to us." Just remembering it made me want to throw up.

"Maybe it was light tricking you again, like with the seal," said Rokshar, trying to make me feel better.

"There was a lot of noise and bubbling waves," Max said to her.

"It might have been a sea lion. They can be over seven hundred pounds," she said. "Asim, are you okay?"

"Yes—just surprised," I said. I could barely hear myself over the thundering of my heart.

We boarded the bus. I sighed with relief when it pulled away.

As we left the parking lot, Nelson said, "Do you mind if Max and I get off, Mx. Hudson? The bus is making me feel sicker. I can get a ride back with one of my coworkers."

Our teacher nodded.

"If it's okay, Asim and I will get off, too," said my dad. "I also feel sick."

"No problem," said Mx. Hudson. "Feel better soon, both of you."

"Thanks," said Dad. "Asim, let's go."

Go? I thought. *Back to the water's edge*

and the creatures lurking underneath? My legs did their overcooked noodle impression, but Dad appeared gray and weak. I stood up.

"If you see anything weird," said Rokshar, "write it down and tell me."

I nodded, then forced myself off the bus.

"I need some air," said Nelson. He walked to the dock. Captain Hoxha was there, staring at the water. She looked worried but smiled when she saw us.

"My ears are ringing," said Nelson.

"Did you get water in them?" asked Captain Hoxha.

He shook his head and pressed his finger against his ear.

"When we get home," said Max, "you should lie down."

Nelson winced. "It's getting louder."

Captain Hoxha glanced at my dad and noticed his clammy skin. "Why don't I drive you all home?"

"Can you hear that?" asked Dad, turning in a circle.

"Are you hearing the ringing, too?" I asked.

"No," Dad said, "it's . . . singing. . . ."

"Singing?" I asked. Max and I looked at each other. We were the only people here.

The captain's eyes clouded with unease. When she looked over the water, her mouth tightened.

"Was the boat attacked?" I asked.

She didn't answer me. "Let's get you home," she said, hustling the men toward the research center.

"I hear singing, too," said Nelson, pulling away. "Can't you hear it?"

Max shook his head. So did I.

Captain Hoxha cast an anxious glance at the sea.

"Dad." I stretched out my trembling hand. "Come with me."

"Why can't you hear it?" asked Dad.

"It's louder over here." Nelson pointed to the end of the dock and started walking toward it.

Worry flashed across Max's face. "Stop!"

Fear skittered along my spine.

Captain Hoxha hurried after Nelson.

"That voice," said Nelson. "It's so lovely!" He broke into a run.

"Uncle Nelson, no!" screamed Max.

Nelson threw himself into the water.

Captain Hoxha dived in after him.

"That singing," said Dad. He rushed to the dock's edge.

Max and I hauled him back.

"I have to get to the music!" Dad struggled to break free. He slipped and fell backward. His head thumped on the wooden planks.

"Are you okay?" I helped him sit up.

He rubbed the back of his head. He blinked a few times. "What's happening? Where are Nelson and Captain Hoxha?"

"In the water," said Max, his voice thin. "My uncle jumped in."

"What?!" Dad sprang to his feet, winced, then started for the end of the dock. "That's dangerous!"

We followed. I was ready to grab him, but he stopped at the water's edge.

"I've got him!" Captain Hoxha yelled from the water.

Dad flopped on his belly and crawled forward. When he was hanging over the end, he shouted, "Boys, hold my feet!"

We did, and Dad reached out as far as he could.

Captain Hoxha swam to the ladder, then pushed Nelson onto it. Dad grabbed hold of Nelson and hauled him up. Then he helped the captain. The adults collapsed on the dock.

"What happened?" asked Nelson. "Why was I in the water?"

"You jumped in," said Max. "You said you heard singing. So did Mr. MacInroy. But the rest of us didn't hear anything."

"The last I remember, there was a ringing in my ears," said Nelson.

"I'm calling the ambulance," said Captain Hoxha. "You two need to get checked out."

Max and I locked eyes. There was something scary in Lion's Gate, something that wanted to pull Dad and Nelson under the water.

4

"**W**hat did the doctors say?" asked Rokshar. We were in my room. Max and his mom were taking care of his uncle.

"Seasickness can cause dizziness and headaches," I said. "They think Nelson got confused and fell off the dock."

Rokshar frowned.

"I hypothesized that the lady under the water was a selkie because of the seal," I said, frowning. "But if she was a siren, that would explain everything. Sirens lure people by singing. Their songs can drive

folks to do strange things. Part of the sci-entific method is making observations. Based on what I saw, I'm going to change my hypothesis."

"Remember that harmful algal bloom?" said Rokshar. "Usually, algal blooms are fine. They're a food source for animals. But when a bloom becomes a HAB—a harmful algal bloom— they can be dangerous. HABs have biotoxins that can hurt humans and animals. My hypothesis is that a HAB is responsible for the strange behaviors of your dad and Nelson." She took out her journal and started writing. "We should record this, and we should investigate."

I added another question to my journal.

Was the ghostly figure we saw last week the same woman who was under the water?

I added my new hypothesis.

Sirens are water creatures that lure people to their doom by singing to them. The woman is a siren, and she's connected to what's happening to my dad and Nelson. (Was she behind the attack on the boat? Why does she want them?)

Rokshar squeezed my arm. "Don't worry. We'll figure this out."

Having Rokshar and Max on my side made me feel better. Having Dad at home *really* made me feel better. He was away from the water and safe from whatever creepy thing was there.

That night, a soft thumping woke me. I sat up, trying to clear sleep from my brain. I climbed out of bed and opened the door. The thumping sounded once more. It was coming from downstairs.

I went down the steps and saw Dad. His back was to me. He was walking into the front door, stumbling back, then walking into it over and over.

"Dad?"

He didn't answer.

I heard my parents' bedroom door click open upstairs. Mom came down, throwing on her robe. "Oh dear," she said when she saw Dad. "Someone's sleepwalking again."

"Sleepwalking?" I echoed.

She nodded and quietly moved to Dad. "He used to sleepwalk when he was younger, but he hasn't done it in ages."

"I've never seen Dad sleepwalk," I said. My stomach bubbled with worry.

"It's okay, sweetheart," said Mom. "He'll be fine. It just happens sometimes."

"But after today—" I started to say.

"Stress can affect it," she said. She slowly turned Dad around.

I jerked back. His eyes were open but glazed over.

"We have to be gentle," Mom said. "No loud noises as we guide him back to bed." She grinned. "I'll stay up and make sure the Sandman doesn't get him."

Like me, Mom loved spooky stories—especially the ones she'd heard when she was growing up in Guyana. Unlike me, she thought they were just stories.

"Fret not," she said, helping Dad up the steps. "He'll be fine."

My gut said it wasn't a coincidence that Dad was sleepwalking right after he'd heard singing. It said he was trying to return to the sea. Something in the water wanted him. I stood straight. The sea terrified me, but I wasn't going to let it hurt Dad or Nelson.

When I got back to my room, I emailed my friends.

> I asked Mom if she would take me to the research center tomorrow. She said yes. Want to come?

They replied the next morning, YES! Rokshar's mom and her brothers, Malachi and Devlin, would join us as well.

After school, Mrs. Kaya and my mom took us to the research center. They went inside.

"Rokshar told us spooky stuff might be going down," said Malachi, pulling his dreads out of the way as he zipped his jacket. "We're here to help. Where do we start?"

"I want to test the algae," said Rokshar. She pulled on a pair of gloves and headed to the cliffs. We followed. There was a man looking at the bloom. He smiled at us.

Rokshar gestured to the red tide. "We think this might be a harmful algal bloom. Are we right?"

"We recommend you stay away," he said. "We're treating it with a combination of modified clay particles and seawater.

When the clay sinks to the ground, it will take any harmful cells with it and clear up the water." He waved and walked away.

"So is that a yes?" Max asked.

Devlin shrugged as Rokshar leaned down to collect a sample.

As we walked back to the research center, I told them about Dad's sleepwalking.

"I hope Uncle Nelson is okay," said Max. "I'd hate to think of him sleepwalking."

"Asim's mom said Mr. MacInroy was a sleepwalker before yesterday," said Rokshar. "It might not be connected to the algae."

Just then, I spotted a woman waist-deep in the waves. She was tall, with a narrow face and long brown hair. It looked like she was searching for something. "That's her!" I hissed. "That's the woman who was under the water, following us!"

5

"**W**hat do we do?" asked Max.

"Talk to her," said Rokshar. "We'll ask why she's at the research center and if she was around yesterday. Then we can talk about the algae and see if the HAB is connected to what happened with Nelson and Mr. MacInroy. That will help us figure out which of our hypotheses is correct."

She walked over to the water, and we followed.

The woman spotted us.

The closer we got to her, the more

nervous I became. Sea waves curled on the shore and left bubbling froth. The lady's face was wary and hard. My muscles twitched. We stopped in front of her.

"I saw you following us under the water," I blurted out. I winced as my friends stared at me.

The woman stared, too. It was a long, heart-thumping moment. Then she smiled, the lines of her face softened, and she giggled. "Yes," she said. "That was me."

I didn't trust the smile. It was too big and bright.

"My name is Morgan," she said. "I work here at the center. Yesterday, I was collecting samples and saw your boat. I couldn't resist playing a little joke on you."

"Why were you in the sea?" asked Rokshar. "Why are you collecting samples?"

Morgan's sunny smile flickered. "For my research, among other things."

"Like what?" asked Rokshar.

Her smile flickered even more. "You ask a lot of questions."

"I want to be a scientist," Rokshar said smoothly. She pointed at the cliff. "There's red tide on the other side. Are you studying it?"

"Shouldn't you kids be with your chaperones?" Morgan asked, moving deeper into the water. "I'm quite busy."

"You look like you're searching for something," I said. Morgan made me nervous, but I wouldn't let her ignore us. My dad and Nelson were in trouble, and we needed answers. "Can we help?"

"I'm checking for any seaweed or algae washing up on the shore," she said.

"Like the algae from around the cliff-side?" Rokshar asked.

"Ah! Someone new for you to talk to," said Morgan as a black truck drove into the lot. "So long!"

Max's eyebrows pulled together in worry. "That's Uncle Nelson." His forehead became smooth again. "Maybe he's back to work because he feels better!" He ran to the vehicle as Nelson climbed out.

Morgan froze. "He's one of the men who were here yesterday." She moved toward the shore. Then she stopped and stared at her feet.

Did she find what she was looking for? I wondered. I pulled Rokshar, Devlin, and Malachi away from Morgan. "Did you see how weird she got when we asked about the algae? And she admitted she was near the boat yesterday. She's up to something."

As Nelson and Max came over, Malachi asked, "Why would anyone mess around with harmful algal blooms? Aren't they toxic?"

"Some toxic substances can be useful," said Rokshar. "Foxglove is a dangerous plant. But if it's processed properly, it can help people with irregular heartbeats." She frowned. "But scientists would grow the algae in a lab." She tapped her chin. "The man from the center said they were treating the bloom. . . ." Rokshar trailed off, then looked at Morgan. "Do you think she's growing a HAB without permission?"

I opened my mouth to answer, but Devlin nudged me and said, "Nelson, you look terrible."

Good save. Until we had evidence of a spooky event or science run wild, it was better not to talk about it in front of the adults.

"I'm feeling better," said Nelson. "I wanted some sea air."

He didn't look better. Nelson's face was flushed, and his skin was clammy.

Malachi leaned into me. "He should be at home," he said. "I'm going to find our moms." Malachi left.

Morgan yawned and stretched.

Nelson's eyes turned glassy. He walked toward her.

"Uncle Nelson, come back," Max said, panicking. "Your pants will get wet!"

Nelson ignored him and kept walking.

Devlin tapped Max on top of his head. "Think of a better way to stop him."

Nelson stopped at the water's edge. "My name's Nelson," he said.

"My name's Morgan," she said.

She gestured for him to come closer.

I gasped as he stepped toward the water. "Nelson, no!"

Morgan reached out to grab him, then stumbled back as she saw Mom, Malachi, and Mrs. Kaya running over.

"Nelson!" Mrs. Kaya called sharply. "What are you doing?"

Nelson jerked back. He swooned and clutched his head.

Mrs. Kaya took Nelson by the arm. "Let's get you home."

"I want to talk to the lady!" He tried to pull free, but Mrs. Kaya was stronger.

"There's no one here but us." She herded him to his car. Max followed.

Rokshar and I glanced at the sea, but Morgan had disappeared into the waves.

"Let's go, kids," Mom said.

I started for the car, then looked back. Morgan's face was out of the water. She was making a low, growling sound and staring at Nelson like a hungry animal. The water around her bubbled.

6

The next day, we headed to Max's house. "I'm not kidding," I told Rokshar, Devlin, and Malachi as we climbed the steps to Max's front door. "She looked like she wanted to eat Nelson!"

"Don't tell Max that," Rokshar said, knocking on the door. "He's worried enough. I ran some tests on the water. Last night, the water was acidic, but this morning, it wasn't. Step three of the scientific process is collecting data." She shook her head. "But in this case, the data keeps changing."

"Mom's taking Uncle Nelson to the hospital," Max said as he opened the door. "He's getting worse."

Just then, Nelson strode toward us from the kitchen. "I'm fine. I want to talk to the nice lady. She was here, but you scared her!"

Ms. Rogers sighed. "I told you, there was no one outside your window." She smiled at Rokshar's brothers. "Thank you for staying with Max and his friends." Ms. Rogers guided Nelson out the door.

Max sank to the floor. "Uncle Nelson keeps trying to get out of the house. He's positive Morgan was here, but Mom and I didn't see anyone."

"Maybe it's the HAM thing Rokshar was talking about," said Devlin.

Rokshar sighed. "It's HAB."

What if she was wrong? The thought of my dad being under Morgan's spell made my skin prickle. "Both Nelson and my dad

said they heard singing. That's how sirens get into a person's brain."

"I bet that bump on your dad's head broke Morgan's spell over him." Max shivered. "Good thing she didn't touch Uncle Nelson."

"Microscopic algae can produce biotoxins that get passed to humans if they eat shellfish. It can cause tremors, memory loss, even comas," Rokshar said. "Nelson and Mr. MacInroy didn't have shellfish. But if it's a modified type of HAB, maybe there are new ways it can get into the human body. And there could be different symptoms, like hearing singing." She tilted her head. "Morgan hid when our moms came over. That was suspicious." Rokshar wrote the information in her journal.

I took out my journal and added:

When Morgan yawned, Nelson's eyes went glassy. Was she singing, but only he could hear? Plus, after she introduced herself, she tried to pull him into the water. Why? And why wouldn't she get out of the water?

I stopped. Something about my entry was tickling my brain. I reread my notes. "Wait! Morgan said that she worked for the center, but she introduced herself to Nelson. If she was really working there, wouldn't she already know him?"

"There's only one way to find out." Rokshar set down her notebook. "Let's go there and get some answers!"

We got permission to go to the research center. Then my friends and I rushed to the pier.

"There's Captain Hoxha," said Rokshar as we locked our bikes.

We ran over to her. I said, "The boat was attacked, wasn't it? That's why you didn't want us on the water."

She squinted at the horizon. "It's not safe to be on the water. That's all I'm going to say." The captain walked away.

"Wait." Rokshar caught up to her. "We met a woman named Morgan who says she works for the center. Do you know her?"

Captain Hoxha went very still. "I don't know her, but we've hired a lot of new people." She refused to look at us.

She's hiding something, I thought.

Judging by the expressions on my

friends' faces, they were thinking the same thing.

"Don't go near the water," Captain Hoxha said sternly, then left.

"That was a waste of time," said Max.

Malachi pointed. "Maybe not. Look."

Morgan was on the deck of the boat. She crouched when she saw the captain, then watched her.

"Hide!" said Malachi.

Max ducked behind Devlin.

Malachi sighed. "Hide better!"

"Follow me," said Rokshar. Staying low, she led us off the pier and hid behind a dinghy.

We peered around it.

Captain Hoxha went to the doors of the building. She stopped, then spun to face the boat.

Morgan ducked.

"No way is Morgan working for the center," Rokshar whispered.

"So what's she doing here?" asked Devlin.

"Growing the HAB." Rokshar closed her eyes. "New HAB symptoms,

strange water readings . . ." She opened her eyes. "What if Morgan is from a rival lab and she's using Lion's Gate as part of her HAB-growing experiment? Tonight, I'm going to add that to my hypothesis."

The captain went into the research center.

Morgan stood. She limped away and disappeared around the corner of the wheelhouse.

Limping? The thought pinged my brain, but I couldn't figure out why.

When Morgan reappeared, she was in the water by the boat. She put her hands on the hull, then pulled them away. She stared at them.

"It's the algae," whispered Rokshar.

Morgan licked her fingers, then winced.

"Gross," said Devlin. "I'm never eating again!"

Morgan sank beneath the water.

We raced onto the pier, looking for her.

Devlin scanned the sea, then pointed. "There!" Morgan was swimming toward the red tide. She disappeared, then reappeared next to the HAB. We watched as she threaded her fingers through the red water. Morgan pressed her palm against her neck and sank beneath the waves.

We paced the shore, waiting for her to surface.

Devlin chewed his nail. "Maybe I should get Captain—"

Just then, Morgan appeared. We stared in shock. She was so far out to sea we could barely see her.

"How did she hold her breath for so long?" Malachi asked.

"There are professional divers who can hold their breath underwater for a long time," said Rokshar. "But she pressed her neck, remember? Maybe it's a new type of breathing device."

Behind us, a car horn sounded. Dad turned into the parking lot. He walked over and said, "I was driving home when I spotted you! Do you want a ride?"

"We're okay. We brought our bikes," I said, casting a worried glance back at the water. Morgan had tried to grab hold of Nelson. Even if she was far out to sea, I didn't want Dad near the water. "You should head home."

Dad looked at the sand. "There's something shining. . . . It might be a coin." He bent down to grab the object. As he stepped forward, the waves washed over his shoes. Dad jerked upright, then collapsed as a piercing shriek echoed over the water.

7

I stood in the doorway of my parents' bedroom.

"The doctor thinks you caught a virus," Mom said as she tucked blankets around Dad in bed.

"I didn't feel sick," he said. "I was fine, then I stepped in the water. . . ."

The water that Morgan was swimming in. I was sure she was the one who'd screamed. The shrill sound echoed in my ears. I took Dad's hand and tried to calm my racing heart.

Mom brushed my hair with her fingers. "Why don't we let him get some rest?"

I nodded and went to my room. There was an email from Rokshar to everyone.

I looked at the algae sample under the microscope. It has a microalgae group that causes an illness called Amnesic Shellfish Poisoning. This can cause short-term memory loss in humans, but it doesn't explain why Nelson and Mr. MacInroy heard singing. I also found another algae group I can't identify. Is Morgan mixing different types of algae? I wonder if this type emits a gas that messes with hearing. I'm putting all this information in my journal and will keep testing.

Rokshar wasn't the only one with new information. I got my journal and wrote:

Morgan is behind the weird things happening to Dad and Nelson. I thought she might be a siren. But Nelson had talked about seeing Morgan outside his window. Sirens can't come onto land . . . can they?

Setting down my journal, I went to a stack of notebooks. In them, Mom and I had collected all the supernatural stories we'd heard. I flipped through the pages, looking for an answer. I didn't find one, but I read something important. In ancient times, sailors would block out a siren's call by putting beeswax in their ears.

I went dizzy with relief. Getting Dad and Nelson earplugs would save them! Rushing to my computer, I emailed my friends. A few minutes later, Rokshar replied.

> If Morgan is a siren, this is great information! But if my hypothesis is correct—that Morgan's with another lab—it might explain the boat attack. And why the captain doesn't want anyone near the water. PS. Morgan touched the algae, then licked her fingers. This might make her sick.

"Asim, could you bring a glass of water to your dad?" called Mom.

"Coming!" I sped to the kitchen, then skidded to a horrified stop.

On the other side of the window was Morgan. Her fingernails had become long, sharp talons, and she was using them to try to cut a hole in the glass.

She saw me. Her eyes bugged out, and when she opened her mouth, her teeth were fangs. "Give me back what's mine," she said.

"I'm not giving you my dad!" I wanted to get Mom, but my legs were frozen.

She howled. It was the same high-pitched shriek I heard at the sea. The window rattled. I covered my ears.

"Give me what is mine," she said. "Or I'll take what you love!"

"Asim!" Mom yelled from upstairs. "What's going on?"

Morgan jerked at Mom's voice. She hissed, then turned and fled across the lawn.

Anger broke my terror. She had tried to steal my dad! I threw open the back door and chased her. Morgan sped into the forest. She was fast, but she was hobbling. I put on speed, trying to catch her. The night was dark and foggy. It was hard to see her.

I stopped, panting for breath. Then

I caught sight of her shadowy figure. I went after her. Tree roots jutted out of the ground. I stumbled over them but didn't fall. Moonlight broke through the branches and highlighted Morgan in silver. She tripped over some brambles, then limped toward the clearing. I chased her back onto the street.

Morgan turned the corner.

I sped after her, but she'd disappeared into the mist. She wouldn't be the only one limping tonight. I'd hurt my calf chasing after her. *Wait a second.* Maybe *limping* wasn't the right word. It was more

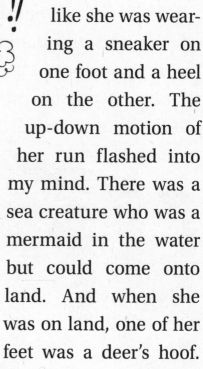

like she was wearing a sneaker on one foot and a heel on the other. The up-down motion of her run flashed into my mind. There was a sea creature who was a mermaid in the water but could come onto land. And when she was on land, one of her feet was a deer's hoof. I knew what Morgan was, and it left me dizzy with fear. She was far more dangerous than we'd thought.

"It was terrifying," I told my friends when we met at Rokshar's house the next day. "I thought her scream would shatter the glass!"

"You thought she was a siren," said Malachi. "But they only live in the water."

"My hypothesis was wrong." I sat down. "She's not a siren. Her run gave her away. She's a fairmaid. They're from the Caribbean. They're a type of mermaid that can come onto land. Some people say one foot of a fairmaid is a deer hoof. That explains her unusual way of running."

"Or maybe she hurt herself," said Rokshar.

"Why do you look so worried?" Devlin asked me.

That was the question I was dreading. "Fairmaids are really dangerous," I said, taking out my

notebook. "Some of the stories say they'll steal a person's shadow and leave them senseless."

Max covered his face.

Devlin put his arm around Max's shoulders.

"There has to be a way to stop Morgan," said Malachi.

"I don't think it's about stopping her," said Rokshar. "We don't have any real evidence that she's a fairmaid—"

"Look at what's happening," said Malachi. "She's involved!"

"I agree, but think about it scientifically," she said. "Morgan's been swimming in the water near the algae. She licked some of it! We know something is going on with the bloom because the center's using a clay treatment on it." She leaned forward. "Maybe whatever toxin is infecting Nelson and Mr. MacInroy is infecting her, too. If she is experimenting with HABs, she might need a doctor."

I opened my journal and reread my notes. Something was missing. I closed my eyes and thought about the day on the boat . . . Morgan trying to climb onto it . . . the boat getting attacked . . . Dad and Nelson getting sick . . . Morgan trying to grab Nelson and steal my dad . . . fairmaids . . .

My eyes snapped open. "Nelson and Dad were on the beach, picking things up, before we got on the boat." Two memories flashed in my mind: Morgan searching in the water. Later, she was on the boat.

I jumped to my feet. "I bet one of them accidentally took something that belonged to her!" I stuffed my notebook into my bag. "Max, go home. See if your uncle left a comb at your house. The stories say it might be made of gold or have seashells. If my hypothesis is right and she's a fairmaid, that's what she wants. We can use it to stop her. I'm going to check my place, too."

I ran home. Mom was on the couch, sleeping. I tiptoed past her and went to my parents' bedroom. I crept inside. The window was open, and the curtains were blowing in the late-afternoon breeze. Dad was gone.

The phone began to ring, and I thought of Morgan's last words, *Give me what is mine. Or I'll take what you love!*

9

Trembling, I picked up the phone. "Hello?"

It was Max. "Uncle Nelson snuck out of the hospital! Mom's organizing a search party."

I collapsed on the bed. "My dad is missing, too!"

"What do we do?" he cried.

"We help," I said. "I'll talk to my mom. Max, you update Rokshar and her brothers. Let's meet at their place."

I hung up the phone. Then I ran downstairs. I woke Mom up and told her *almost* everything. She grabbed her phone and started calling people to help search. I ran back upstairs and looked through Dad's clothing. I found coins and a necklace.

Then I spotted a haircomb made of sea-shells. A thrill of victory zipped through my body. This was what Morgan wanted, and I was going to use it to protect Lion's Gate from her forever.

Mom dropped me off at Rokshar's. I pulled out the comb. "This is how we defeat her. If you have a fairmaid's comb, she must do what you tell her. I bet she was the ghostly figure we saw last week. She lost the comb—that's why she came back!"

Malachi grinned. "Sweet! We make her give us Nelson and Mr. MacInroy in exchange for it."

Rokshar looked worried. "It'll work if Morgan is a supernatural creature. But what if it's the biotoxin? We need a plan for that, too."

"Her eyes bugged out, and her teeth were fangs," I said to Rokshar. "That's a fairmaid."

"Or the crossbred algae are making her sick," said Rokshar. "If Morgan's mixing dangerous algae types, then maybe her brain is injured. She might believe she's a fairmaid. We can't let her hurt Mr. MacInroy or Nelson or herself."

My gut said Morgan *was* a fairmaid, but Rokshar had a point. We didn't have proof either way. "What do we do?"

"Come to the kitchen. I might have a way to stop her," Rokshar said.

Ten minutes later, we packed spray bottles of tap water into our bags.

"It won't hurt her," said Rokshar, "but getting sprayed with water should distract her long enough for us to rescue Mr. MacInroy and Nelson."

When we arrived at the reseach center, daylight was starting to fade. But it was bright enough for us to see Nelson and my dad stepping into a dinghy.

Malachi pulled out his phone and called his mom.

Nelson untied the rope that moored the boat to the dock.

"Quick! Grab it before they get to open water!" Devlin yelled.

We ran to the dock. The rope slithered away. Max leaped and caught hold of it. We raced to him, then grabbed hold of the rope.

Malachi ran up, tucking his phone into his pocket. "Pull them back to shore!"

We formed a single line and tugged on the rope.

"Let us go!" screamed Dad. "She's calling us!"

Nelson tried to yank the rope from us.

My friends and I pulled harder, and the dinghy floated our way. Suddenly, waves crashed against the hull. The force knocked us off our feet and threw Dad and Nelson to their knees.

Max lost hold of the rope. I did, too. We scrambled back to our feet and caught hold of it in the growing twilight.

Morgan's shadowy form appeared in the water beside the boat. She pulled at the edge of the stern. The boat jerked toward the open sea. Nelson and Dad grabbed hold of the rope and yanked. It made the boat rock. They let go and sat down.

My friends and I kept pulling. My fingers were growing numb. It was getting harder to hold on.

We heaved, digging in our heels, and yanked with all our might. My muscles vibrated from the effort. Slowly, the boat floated to the pier. Malachi and Devlin tied the rope to a post.

Morgan screamed in frustration. "Give me what is mine!"

Nelson and Dad howled and covered their ears.

"I have what you want, Morgan!" I cried. "I have the comb!"

"Give it to me!" She ran through the shallow water. The waves churned.

I reached into my pocket, but the comb was gone! "It must have fallen out of my pocket!" I said to Max and Rokshar.

I dropped to my knees and began feeling around the pier.

"Time's up," hissed Morgan. "I will take what you love."

"No!" I screamed.

She stood still in the water and opened her mouth, like she was yawning. I didn't hear anything, but Dad and Nelson began to sway side to side.

"Got it!" Max held up the comb.

"Run to the research center!" I yelled to him.

I raced with him. Morgan shrieked and chased us.

"Toss it to me!" I held out my hands.

Max threw the comb.

I spun around. "Stop or I'll break it!"

She froze.

"Now!" I yelled at Rokshar, Max,

Devlin, and Malachi. They grabbed the bottles from Rokshar's bag, aimed the nozzles, and sprayed Morgan.

She screamed. "It's burning!"

"It's just tap water," cried Rokshar. "It can't hurt you!"

Morgan launched herself at me and tried to grab the comb.

"I know the rules!" I held it tight. "You have to do what I say because I have the comb. Leave Lion's Gate and never come back!"

Morgan wrenched the comb away from me and ran into the sea.

"Get her!" cried Rokshar. "She needs help!"

We raced after her, but Morgan disappeared beneath the waves.

The next morning, my friends and I stood on the shore, along with Ms. Rogers, Mrs. Kaya, and my mom, watching the boats search for Morgan.

"I heard security guards talking," said Malachi. He spoke quietly so our parents wouldn't hear. "They think Morgan had a small submarine and was using it to ram the boat the other day."

"That would explain the scratches on the hull," said Rokshar, "and the boat attack."

Maybe, I thought, but I remembered how strong Morgan was. She could have attacked the boat herself.

My dad and Nelson came over.

Nelson rubbed the back of his head. "I can't remember anything."

Dad nodded in agreement.

Mom hugged him. "I'm glad both of you are feeling better."

The adults wandered off. My friends and I went to the end of the dock.

"Do you think Morgan was from a rival lab?" Max asked.

Rokshar nodded. "It explains why they can't find her. She escaped in her submarine." She frowned. "But it doesn't explain her weird reaction to the tap water . . . unless it was a side effect of her HAB infection."

"Or she was a fairmaid," said Malachi. "The sea is salty. Fresh water could have felt like it was burning."

Rokshar nodded at the cliffside. "The clay destroyed the bloom, but you know what's weird? The sample I had is gone, too. When I looked this morning, it was just seawater." She sighed. "Part of the scientific process is being able to repeat the tests. Since the samples are gone, I can't prove my hypothesis about the algae."

I stepped away from my friends to

the dock's edge. "Remember the rules," I said to the water. It began to bubble. "You can never come back to Lion's Gate again."

The water bubbled more, frothed, then settled.

"Whoa," said Malachi. "That's weird."

"Not really," said Rokshar as a seal poked its head out of the water. It barked at us and disappeared under the waves. My friends turned away. So did I, but not before I caught sight of a green fish tail and long brown hair.

"Asim," said Max, "what are you thinking?"

"Do you think it's true," I asked, "that some docks float on water because of *pier pressure*?"

My friends groaned.

I laughed.

Notes from Rokshar's Journal

- I'm puzzled by the strange case of Morgan and the algae. Asim's hypothesis about Morgan being a fairmaid fits the events. But the events also fit my hypothesis that Morgan was a spy from another lab, trying to grow a new type of red tide / HAB. I believe the biotoxins from this bloom negatively affected her, Nelson, and Mr. MacInroy.

- Is it possible the algae near the cliffside were modified? Did it make the adults hear and see things that weren't there?

- Stranger still, the disappearance of the microscopic algae from my sample. I have no answers to this puzzling twist. Nor can I explain

Sample

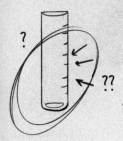
? ?? why, after the HAB disappeared, Nelson and Mr. MacInroy immediately recovered.

- And what of Morgan? Did she use a submarine to escape the island? Is that why there is no trace of her?

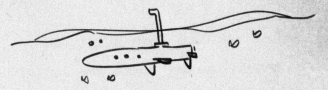

- I'm left with no proof for either Asim's theory or mine. Conclusion: I cannot say whether Morgan is a Fairmaid or a spy.

Spy?

Notes from Asim's Journal

* Morgan is a fairmaid.

* Morgan said she worked at the research center, but there is no record of her there or at the lab.

* Only Dad and Nelson were affected by her. Whenever she was around, they acted strangely.

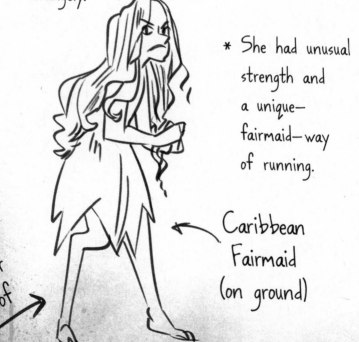

* She had unusual strength and a unique— fairmaid—way of running.

Caribbean Fairmaid (on ground)

Deer hoof →

* The day Dad stepped into the water and she was in it, he collapsed.

* Morgan told me to give her back what was hers—the comb.

Seashell comb

* When I tested my hypothesis that Morgan was a fairmaid, by holding the comb and telling her she could never return, she disappeared. Since then, no one has seen her.

* Conclusion: There is no doubt in my mind that Morgan is a fairmaid and that my friends and I saved Dad and Nelson.

Need new spray bottles

Author's Note

Tales of fairmaids have a special—and creepy—place in my family. Many of my ancestors and elders claimed to have had direct, spooky contact with them.

As a kid, I was told to avoid the water at night because it belonged to the fairmaids. They didn't like humans and were protective of their water. If you upset them, they would follow you onto land!

The only way to defeat a fairmaid was to take hold of her comb and command her to do your bidding. But fairmaids were also protective of their combs, and they would never let them out of their sight.

What would have happened to Nelson and Mr. MacInroy if Asim hadn't found the comb? Perhaps, when it comes to Lion's Gate and the sea, Captain Hoxha's advice is best: don't go near the water!

GET A SNEAK PEEK AT
THE NEXT BOOK IN THE
SPOOKY SLEUTHS SERIES.

Turn the page . . . if you dare!

"Goodness!" said Ms. Rogers when she opened the door. She eyed the dirt on my clothes. "Asim, what happened?"

"I fell," I said, and stepped inside.

"You poor thing," she said. "I'll make some hot chocolate. That'll get you warm."

I cleaned up and changed into my pajamas, then met my friends in Max's room.

"Did you really fall?" asked Malachi, brushing his dreads off his forehead. "Or did you run into something spooky?"

"Both," I said. "I fell into a hole behind one of the abandoned houses."

Max's blue eyes went wide. "What were you doing there?"

I told them what happened.

Devlin hugged his thin frame. "Those houses are creepy. I bet you saw a ghost. They're just air; that's why it couldn't help you."

"Then who threw the rope down for him?" asked Rokshar.

Devlin's cheeks puffed out. "A helpful ghost with telekinetic powers."

"A ghost that can move things with its mind?" Max clutched his mug. "That's worse than a regular ghost!"

"Did you write it down in your journal?" Rokshar asked me.

She and I had been keeping a record

of all the spooky things we ran into. "Not yet," I said, "but I will."

Rokshar moved to the computer and pulled her purple hair into a ponytail. "The fireball is weird. So is the hole spontaneously closing up." She started typing.

We watched over her shoulder. She tried different search terms, like "glowing ball in Lion's Gate" and "meteorite hole closing," but she didn't have any luck. "There's only one thing we can do."

"Pretend it never happened?" Max said hopefully.

"No," she said. "We investigate. Monday, after school."

Max groaned. "I was afraid you'd say that."

Sunday night, before bed, I pulled out my journal. Step one of the scientific process was to ask a question.

A glowing ball of fire appeared in the sky and landed behind the row of abandoned houses. What was it? How did the hole disappear so quickly?

I pulled up my socks, then added:

I fell into the hole. Why were the sides warm and smooth?

I had a lot of guesses. The fireball might be something supernatural, a meteorite, space junk, or an alien ship. Step two of the scientific process was to form a hypothesis. But there were too many options for just one. I climbed into bed.

The next morning, I had breakfast with my parents.

"Do you want a slice of toast?" asked Dad, holding up a bag of bread.

"No thanks," I said.

"But it *loafs* you," he said.

Mom and I groaned.

"I'm going to school," I said.

"So early?" Mom asked, checking her watch.

"Uh, yeah. I'm going to hang out with my friends before the bell," I said.

"Hmm." She gave me a suspicious look but let me go.

I left to find some clues about the fire-ball. I turned the corner and saw a lady standing in front of the same abandoned house where I'd been on Saturday.

Her long black hair blew in the wind as she scanned the upper floors. She started for the porch.

"Wait!" I called. "It's not safe!" But I was too far away. She couldn't hear me. I sped along the icy sidewalk, looking down to avoid the slippery bits. When I got to the walkway that led up to the house, the lady had disappeared.

I went to the back of the house, but she wasn't there. A creepy-crawly feeling slithered along my neck. I wanted to bolt, but what if the lady was in trouble? I retraced my steps. There were no foot-prints leading to the door. *At least she didn't go inside,* I thought, relieved. *That would have been dangerous!*

Dread filled my body as I realized that there were no footprints anywhere, except for mine.

I got to school just as the final bell rang.

"Cutting it close," said Mx. Hudson as I scurried into the classroom. They smiled, so I knew I wasn't in trouble.

I hurried to my desk. Rokshar sat across from me, and Max was behind her. I told them what had happened. "Who doesn't leave footprints in the snow?"

"Ghosts," Max said.

"After school," whispered Rokshar, "we'll investigate."

"I have a special surprise for you all," said Mx. Hudson as someone knocked on our classroom door. "You're going to love it."

I hated it when adults said that. They were never right.

WANT MORE MYSTERY, SCIENCE, AND ADVENTURE?

Check out these chapter book series!

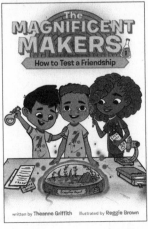

New friends. New adventures.
Find a new series ... just for you!

1220b

rhcbooks.com